S

An I CAN READ Book

RAT IS DEAD AND ANT IS SAD

Based on a Pueblo Indian tale

BETTY BAKER

Pictures by

MAMORU FUNAI

Harper & Row, Publishers

Library of Congress Cataloging in Publication Data
Baker, Betty.
   Rat is dead and ant is sad (based on a Pueblo Indian tale)

(An I can read book)
   SUMMARY: A cumulative tale of the events
occurring after Ant mistakenly announces that Rat
is dead.
   1. Pueblo Indians—Legends. 2. Indians of
North America—Southwest, New—Legends.
[1. Pueblo Indians—Legends. 2. Indians of
North America—Legends] I. Funai, Mamoru.
II. Title.
E99.P9B14 1981   398.2'08997 [E]   78-19483
ISBN 0-06-020346-3
ISBN 0-06-020347-1 (lib. bdg.)

RAT IS DEAD AND ANT IS SAD

Rat had a knot in his fur.

He bit and pulled

but could not get it out.

"Ant will help," he said,

and he went to find her.

Ant was in the cookhouse

picking up seeds

and bits of corn.

"I have a knot in my fur,"

Rat told her.

"Turn around," said Ant.

"I will take it out."

"What is in the pot?" said Rat.

But Ant was busy

and could not say.

Rat got up to look.

He looked and leaned

farther and farther.

"The knot is out," said Ant,

and she let go.

PLOP went Rat.

"Rat," said Ant,

"do you need help?

Rat," said Ant,

"are you still alive?"

But Rat was busy

and could not say.

Ant ran this way and that.

Then she began to cry.

"Why do you cry?"

said Jay.

"Rat is dead

and I am sad," said Ant.

"That is why I cry."

"I will be sad, too,"

said Jay.

"I will drop my feathers."

He did.

And he fell into a cottonwood tree.

"Where are your feathers?"

said the cottonwood tree.

"Rat is dead

and Ant is sad

and so I dropped my feathers,"

said Jay.

"If Rat is dead

and Ant is sad

and you have no feathers,

I will shrivel and shrink,"

said the tree.

And it did.

A sheep came to the cottonwood tree.

It came to get out of the sun,

but the tree gave no shade.

"Why are you small and shriveled?"

said the sheep.

"Rat is dead

and Ant is sad

and Jay dropped his feathers.

That is why I shriveled,"

said the cottonwood tree.

"If Rat is dead

and Ant is sad

and Jay has no feathers

and you shriveled and shrank,

I will grow thin," said the sheep.

And she did.

She went to the river to drink.

The river said,

"Why so thin, sheep?"

The sheep said,

"Rat is dead and Ant is sad.

Jay has no feathers

and the cottonwood shriveled

and shrank.

That is why I am thin."

"If that is so," said the river,

"I will run dry."

And the river did.

A girl came to get water.

"Why are you dry?"

she said to the river.

"Rat is dead and Ant is sad.

Jay dropped his feathers,

the cottonwood shriveled,

and the sheep grew thin.

That is why I am dry,"

said the river.

"Then I will break my jar,"

said the girl.

And she did.

Her mother said,

"Where is the water?"

The girl told her,

"Rat is dead

and Ant is sad.

Jay dropped his feathers

and the cottonwood shriveled

and shrank.

The sheep grew thin

and the river ran dry

and so I broke the water jar."

"And I will burn my earrings,"
said her mother.
And she did.

Her brother said,

"Why do you burn your earrings?"

"Rat is dead

and everyone is sad,"

said the girl's mother.

"That is why I burn my earrings."

"Then I will cut off

my horse's tail,"

said the man.

But the horse would not let him.

The horse said,

"My tail is long and lovely

and it keeps away the flies.

Why do you want to cut it off?"

"Rat is dead

and I am sad," said the man.

"If that is so," said the horse,

"then you must cut off my tail.

But did you see Rat dead?"

"No," said the man.

"I saw my sister

burn her earrings."

"Did you see Rat dead?"

said the horse.

"No," said the woman,

"but my girl saw the river

and it was dry."

The horse went to the river.

"Did you see Rat dead?" she said.

"No," said the river,

"but I saw the sheep

and she was thin."

"Did you see Rat dead?"

said the horse.

"No," said the sheep.

"I saw the cottonwood tree

and now it gives no shade."

The horse went to the tree.

"Did you see Rat dead?" she said.

"No," said the tree.

"I saw Jay

when he fell in me."

"I was sad

and dropped my feathers,"

said Jay.

"Then you saw Rat dead,"

said the horse.

"No," said Jay.

"I saw Ant crying."

The horse went looking for Ant.

Ant was still crying.

"Rat is dead,"

she told the horse.

"Where is he?" said the horse.

"In the pot," said Ant.

"I let him fall in."

The horse looked in the pot.

"That silly ant

didn't look in the pot," she said.

"And I almost lost

my lovely long tail."

Then she turned around

and put her tail

into the pot.

Rat climbed out.

"Rat," said Ant,

"you are still alive!"

She began to run

this way and that

picking up seeds

and bits of corn.

"Rat is back,"

she said.

"We must have a dance."

The horse had knots

in her long lovely tail

but Ant took them out

and Rat helped.

The river ran full

and the sheep grew fat

and the cottonwood soon gave shade.

The woman made jars
and her brother gave her
new blue earrings.

But Jay had to sit

in the tree

for a long, long time

until his feathers grew back.

64